STARS OF SPORT

SHAQUILLE O'NEAL

BY RAYMOND H. MILLER

KIDHAVEN
PRESS™

THOMSON

GALE

San Diego • Detroit • New York • San Francisco • Cleveland
New Haven, Conn. • Waterville, Maine • London • Munich

For more information, contact
KidHaven Press
27500 Drake Rd.
Farmington Hills, MI 48331-3535
Or you can visit our Internet site at http://www.gale.com

LIBRARY OF CONGRESS CATALOGING-IN-PUBLICATION DATA

Miller, Raymond H., 1967–
  Shaquille O'Neal / by Raymond H. Miller.
    p. cm.—(Stars of sport)
Summary: Looks at this basketball star's childhood, his college career, the seasons
he spent with the Orlando Magic, and his dominant play with the Los Angeles
Lakers.
Includes bibliographical references (p.   ) and index.
  ISBN 0-7377-1422-0 (alk. paper)
  1. O'Neal, Shaquille—Juvenile literature. 2. Basketball players—United States—
Biography—Juvenile literature. [1. O'Neal, Shaquille. 2. Basketball players.
3. African Americans—Biography.] I. Title. II. Series.
  GV884.O54 M55 2003
  796.323'092—dc21

2002009465

Printed in the United States of America.

Contents

Center of Attention

Basketball stardom did not come easily for Shaquille O'Neal. Growing up in a military household, he had difficulty making friends because his family moved a lot. Classmates teased him because he was unusually tall. And he was punished frequently by his stepfather for getting bad grades and stealing. He eventually turned his life around and focused on basketball, becoming an **all-American** in college and a National Basketball Association (NBA) number one draft pick.

At seven feet, one inch tall and 315 pounds, O'Neal is among the largest and most dominant players in NBA history. He is a ten-time all-star, an Olympic gold medalist, and a winner of the NBA's

O'Neal happily displays his Most Valuable Player Award after the Los Angeles Lakers won the NBA championship in 2001.

Most Valuable Player (MVP) **Award.** But above all else he is a champion. After trying for eight years to make it to the top, he finally won an NBA championship with the Los Angeles Lakers in 2000. He led the Lakers to titles again in 2001 and 2002.

O'Neal is just as big a star off the basketball court. He records rap albums, acts in movies, and gives generously to charities that benefit children.

CHAPTER ONE

A Big Boy

Shaquille Rashuan O'Neal was born on March 6, 1972, to Lucille O'Neal in Newark, New Jersey. A short time later Shaquille's father, Joe Toney, left Lucille and never returned. As a result Shaquille was given his mother's last name. Times were hard for the O'Neals the first few years of Shaquille's life. Lucille was just out of high school and on welfare, but she soon went to work for the city of Newark to support her son. It was a low-paying job, so she could not afford a home for the two of them. They moved around a lot, living with several different family members in the low-income neighborhoods of Newark. They also lived with his grandmother, Odessa Chambliss, who Shaquille grew to love.

As a baby Shaquille had a large appetite and grew quickly. By the time he could walk he was much larger than most children his age. His mother sensed he was going to be big as an adult as well. Several of Shaquille's ancestors were tall. His great grandfather on his mother's side stood six feet, nine inches, and his grandfather on his father's side was also well above average in height.

Not only was Shaquille large as a toddler, he was also very curious. He picked up everything within reach and was constantly getting into trouble. As a single mom Lucille did the best she could to discipline Shaquille, but he got harder to handle as he grew.

O'Neal was born in Newark, New Jersey, and lived there for several years.

Army Dad

When Shaquille was two years old, his mother met a man her age named Phil Harrison. The two dated a short while, then got married. Shaquille had a hard time accepting his stepfather at first. He was used to getting all the attention and did not like sharing his mother. Eventually Shaquille warmed up to his stepfather and grew to love him. Phil and Lucille later had three children together: Ayesha, Lateefah, and Jamal.

Phil had grown up in poverty and did not want Shaquille to go through the same experience. He decided to join the U.S. Army to provide a better way of

O'Neal receives congratulations from his stepfather, Phil Harrison, after a 2001 victory against the Portland Trail Blazers.

life for his family. Since the military did not pay very well, he worked part-time driving a delivery truck to increase the family income. Phil was a **drill sergeant** in the army and became a very strict father. He tried to teach his stepson right from wrong but had little success. For example, when Shaquille was five years old, he tried to light his teddy bear on fire. The bear did not catch fire, but it smoldered and the house filled with smoke. The incident resulted in one of the many spankings Shaquille received from his stepfather.

Growing up in a military household was not easy for Shaquille because he never had a permanent home. Phil was transferred to several different bases in New Jersey, and the family always moved along with him. Shaquille was often pulled out of school in the middle of the year to move to another base—just as he was making friends.

The one constant thing in Shaquille's boyhood was his love of sports. He often ran around the house with either a football or a basketball in his hands. Football was his favorite sport, but at around age nine that began to change. Phil, who had played college basketball, taught Shaquille the game and gave him shooting tips. Before long Shaquille was dribbling up and down the court and making baskets. He even got to be the ball boy on his stepfather's army basketball team.

No Pass—No Play

Shaquille grew at an amazing rate. By age ten he looked much older than the boys his age. He was so

Jack McCallum (right) of Sports Illustrated *interviews O'Neal after practice.*

big when he started playing sports that the other play-ers' parents complained. They did not believe he was the same age as everyone else. Shaquille's mother sometimes carried his birth certificate with her to prove his age.

Phil and Lucille tried their hardest to keep Shaquille from being embarrassed about his height, but it was no use. He did not like being so much taller than everyone else and just wanted to fit in with the other kids. In the hallways he slouched when he walked to make himself look shorter. Because he was so tall, he was also quite clumsy. His classmates teased him about being awkward and nicknamed him "Shaqsquatch." Eventually the teasing angered him so much that he fought back. Before long Shaquille was known as the school bully. When he moved to a new school he quickly picked a fight with the strongest kid just to prove how tough he was.

Shaquille was also a class clown. He spent most of his time trying to make the other kids laugh, and he rarely paid attention to his teachers. His grades soon began to drop. When he was ten years old he got all Fs on his report card. After school that day he ran to the local arcade to hide, but his stepfather found him. Instead of a spanking, Shaquille received a strong warning to do better in school. His mother decided not to let him play sports until he raised his grades. She called it the "no pass—no play" rule. Though he continued to show behavioral problems outside the classroom, his grades began to improve.

The Move

After living at several different army bases in New Jersey, Shaquille's stepfather was transferred to Georgia. The family lived there only a short time before Phil learned he was being transferred again—this time to a base in West Germany. Shaquille did not want to go. He begged his parents to let him live with his grandmother Odessa in New Jersey. But when the family moved to West Germany, he went with them.

Shaquille was unhappy living overseas and tried to get sent back to the United States by finding more trouble. He pulled a fire alarm on a dare, and he broke into a car to steal cassette tapes. Each time Shaquille did something wrong, his stepfather became more and more furious—sometimes even striking Shaquille. His mom was much more gentle in her approach, and she tried talking to him. But in the end it was Shaquille's fear of being disciplined by his stepfather that made him change his ways.

Also playing a part in Shaquille's turnaround was his love of basketball. The winters in West Germany were too cold and snowy to do anything outdoors, so he spent much of the time in the base gym shooting baskets. He attended an American high school on the base and wanted to join the varsity team, but he was not quite good enough. He was six feet, eight inches tall and could not dunk a basketball. His legs were not strong enough to jump that high.

Dale Brown

Shaquille attended a basketball clinic at the base in hopes of improving. Dale Brown, head coach at Louisiana State University (LSU), was the visiting instructor. He picked Shaquille out of the crowd and

O'Neal clowns around during a workout. He grew to love basketball while living with his family in Germany.

Coach Dale Brown (left) of the Louisiana State Tigers met O'Neal in Germany when he was fourteen years old.

asked him to demonstrate his strength by throwing the ball the length of the court. Shaquille's arms were much stronger than his legs, and he easily threw the ball the entire distance. Brown was impressed. Afterward he talked to Shaquille, who was much taller than the coach. Brown asked Shaquille how long he had been in the army. When Shaquille told him he was only fourteen years old, the coach was amazed. He told Shaquille to study hard and work on his basketball skills so that he might one day be able to play at LSU.

Impact
Player

During Shaquille's sophomore year in high school, the family moved from West Germany to an army base in San Antonio, Texas. Shaquille had grown another three inches and was six feet, eleven inches tall. By then he had embraced his size because he knew it could help him in basketball.

Shaquille made friends at his new high school and talked to them about someday being famous. He even practiced his autograph. Privately, though, he had doubts. So he continued working with his stepfather, who taught him some of the moves used by the greatest **centers** in professional basketball history. He also lifted weights and became much stronger. Under

Phil's supervision Shaquille began to show dramatic improvement.

Any doubts of Shaquille becoming a star were erased his junior year. After strengthening his legs, he could finally dunk. He also used the skills his stepfather taught him to **rebound** the ball. Shaquille was so

O'Neal makes one of his famous dunks during a game against the Southwestern Louisiana Ragin' Cajuns.

big and strong that his teammates simply threw the ball to him and he slam-dunked it. But there was more to Shaquille than dunks and rebounds. He was a good passer and had the speed to run up and down the court with smaller players, something few centers could do.

Shaquille averaged more than seventeen points a game as the team finished the regular season undefeated. They beat several teams in the play-offs before losing in the state championship game. Shaquille took the loss hard, but there was hope for the next year. He was still growing and gaining confidence on the basketball court.

State Champs

Although Shaquille had played well his junior year, he was relatively unknown because of his late start in basketball. He later explained how that changed in his senior year beginning with the Basketball Congress International (BCI) tournament:

> I went to the BCI tournament, one of the show-cases of high-school talent. . . . I'm going into my senior year, only letters I'm getting are from Southwest Texas State and UTSA (University of Texas at San Antonio). . . . I need the big colleges. I want Georgetown. All the coaches are there. Everybody's there. Now it's time to do work. I tore up the competition. Soon as I got home, letters [from the best **Division I** schools] were piling up. For the first time, someone

O'Neal swiftly blocks a shot attempted by a Washington Wizards player.

wrote an article about me. The reporter was talking about all the players. . . . He said I was the best.[1]

After the tournament Shaquille had his choice of Division I colleges, but he quickly narrowed the schools to just one: LSU. He wanted to play for the coach who had helped him at the basketball clinic in West Germany. Before Shaquille's senior season, he committed to LSU.

When Shaquille stepped onto the court as a high school senior, everyone could see why he was going to LSU. He dominated the competition. His dunks were more explosive than ever, and he became an expert at blocking shots. Shaquille averaged more than thirty points a game to lead the team back to the play-offs.

There was no stopping him as the team won the state championship.

Physically Shaquille was ready to play at the next level, but he did not do very well on his college entrance exam. He was in jeopardy of not being accepted by LSU. But when he took another exam, he scored high enough to be admitted.

On to LSU

When Shaquille arrived at the LSU campus in Baton Rouge, Louisiana, he was seventeen years old—one year younger than most freshmen. It was the first time in his life he was separated from his family. But he was mature for a teenager, and his stepfather's many lessons had taught him to be a responsible person. He was ready for the challenges in college—not only in basketball but also in the classroom.

As a business major Shaquille paid close attention in class. He often sat in the front row and asked his professors good questions. He wanted to do well in school because he knew how much his parents wanted him to get a college education. Not wanting to disappoint them, Shaquille studied hard and received good grades.

Shaquille found time to have fun away from class. He showed his playful side by imitating Coach Brown in practice when he was not looking. He also loved to play pranks on his teammates and the other students. The people in his dormitory were the victims of a late-night prank in which he set off fireworks outside the building.

Shaquille got serious when it came to basketball. His backboard-shaking dunks and uncommon quickness for a center amazed his new teammates. Shaquille earned a starting position on the team as a freshman, but his main role was to rebound and play defense. He still performed well enough to be named the Southeast Conference (SEC) Rookie of the Year after averaging more than thirteen points and twelve rebounds a game.

Getting Physical

Shaquille spent much of the summer after his freshman season improving his leaping ability. When he returned to school his sophomore year, he could jump eight inches higher than he could as a freshman. From a standing start he was able to jump and touch a spot on the backboard two and a half feet above the rim. His new leaping ability made him even more difficult to defend under the basket.

LSU's opponents tried to slow Shaquille down by putting two and sometimes three defenders against him. But it was no use. He easily brushed aside defenders and controlled the area close to the basket. His scoring average increased dramatically his second year, and he set a school record with twenty-five "double-doubles" (games in which he scored double-digit points and pulled down double-digit rebounds). He set another LSU record when he scored fifty-three points in a single game. He was named first-team all-American for his outstanding year.

O'Neal nearly sinks a basket during the 1996 Olympics in Atlanta.

Opposing teams used a new strategy against Shaquille during his junior year. They started to **foul** him hard to try to make him miss shots. He was frustrated by the rough play, but he kept his temper under control. In one game late in the season, though, he fought back. While attempting a dunk, a defender

Brian Grant of the Portland Trail Blazers fouls O'Neal during a 2000 Western Conference Finals game.

knocked Shaquille to the floor and would not let him get up. When Shaquille finally got to his feet, he swung at the other player, but missed. The near-fight left an impression on him and his coach. They were afraid a hard foul—or a punch from a fistfight—could possibly cause a severe injury. Not wanting to risk a chance to play in the NBA, Shaquille decided to skip his senior year of college and enter the 1992 draft.

CHAPTER THREE

Magic Man

NBA teams that did not make the play-offs competed in a lottery to decide the draft order, and the team that won the lottery picked first. The 1992 lottery was called "the Shaquille lottery," because every eligible team wanted to draft him. The Orlando Magic, who had finished the 1991–1992 season with a 21-41 record, won the lottery and selected O'Neal.

The Magic were excited to be getting an impact player who could start immediately at the center position. At seven feet, one inch tall and three hundred pounds, O'Neal was among the biggest players in the league. He also wore a size twenty shoe—larger than those worn by other players. In his first game he used his large body to grab eighteen rebounds in a victory over the Miami Heat. But his powerful dunking ability was what made him a star early on in the league. He broke backboards in two separate games while dunking the ball. After that his popularity soared.

O'Neal finished the season averaging 23.4 points a game—eighth most in the league. He received the NBA Rookie of the Year Award for having the best season among first-year players. But more important to O'Neal was Orlando's record. The team finished with forty-one wins—a twenty-game improvement from the last season. They barely missed the play-offs, but with O'Neal on the team the future looked bright.

Shaq Attack!

Companies were attracted to O'Neal because of his huge star appeal. Nicknamed "Shaq," he was one of the few players in professional sports known by one name. He signed commercial endorsement deals with Pepsi and Reebok and quickly became a star off the court. Reebok created a shoe for him called Shaq Attack. They created Shaq Attack T-shirts and posters to promote the shoe. The Shaq Attack logo showed O'Neal in his famous pose: hanging on to the rim during a power dunk.

To promote the Shaq Attack shoe, Reebok sent O'Neal overseas, where he toured Asia, Australia, and Europe. Soon kids around the world were becoming fans of his and buying the Shaq Attack merchandise. He was so popular that extra security guards had to

O'Neal shows off his famous power dunk, a move that attracted the notice of Reebok.

travel with him to keep enthusiastic fans from getting out of control.

O'Neal made a name for himself in other ways outside of basketball. He starred in *Blue Chips*, a movie about a talented high school basketball player trying to make it to college and eventually the NBA. The film did well at the box office and increased his popularity.

O'Neal's success opened doors for him in the entertainment industry. In this picture Shaq performs songs from his album Shaq Diesel.

He also found time to record a rap album and called it *Shaq Diesel*. The album sold more than 1 million copies.

Play-Off Losses

O'Neal did not let his off-court activities affect his play. He was even better his second year, partly because the Magic added another rookie star to the team: Anfernee Hardaway, who started at the guard position. The two complemented each other as Hardaway scored from the outside and O'Neal grabbed rebounds and scored easily in close. Their favorite play was the alley-oop. Hardaway tossed the ball up in the air toward O'Neal, who jumped, grabbed the ball, and dunked it. Orlando fans loved the Hardaway-O'Neal combination.

Even with Hardaway on the team, O'Neal was still the Magic's best player. He averaged nearly thirty points a game as the Magic posted fifty wins to make the play-offs. But the excitement soon faded. Their first-round opponent, the Indiana Pacers, held O'Neal to a season-low fifteen points in Game 2. It did not get any better for him or the Magic as they were swept in four straight games. O'Neal blamed himself for the loss and promised to work harder than ever to improve.

In the 1994–1995 season O'Neal started scoring from the outside, something he did not do very often his first two years in the league. He finally had a jump shot to go with his powerful dunks. With more ways to score, O'Neal led the NBA in points per game with a 29.3 average. He also guided the Magic into the post-season, where they beat three teams in the Eastern

Conference play-offs—including Michael Jordan and the Chicago Bulls—to make the NBA Finals. Matched against the veteran-led Houston Rockets, O'Neal and the Magic were no match. For the second straight year Orlando was swept in four straight games.

Again O'Neal was angry at himself for not leading the team to a championship. Orlando fans and reporters, who usually supported him, blamed him for the loss and said he did not give his best effort. Some people even said he would never win a championship because he was not a good team leader. "Whenever we lost, it was my fault, no matter what I did," he said. "I could have a great, monster play-offs, score 29 [points] a game. But if we didn't win, it was '[You all] got swept and Shaq wasn't playing hard.'" [2]

"Hack-a-Shaq"

O'Neal put the play-off controversy behind him and worked hard on improving his one weakness: shooting **free throws**. His career average was among the league's worst, and teams took advantage by fouling him intentionally. By making him shoot free throws, they often got the ball back when he missed. The strategy became known around the league as "Hack-a-Shaq."

In a preseason game a player from the Miami Heat broke O'Neal's thumb with a hard foul. The Magic star missed the first twenty-two games of the 1995–1996 season. Things got worse once he returned to action. His grandmother, Odessa Chambliss, passed away late in the season. O'Neal had remained close to his grand-

*O'Neal attempts a jump shot over the outstretched arm
of Vlade Divac of the Sacramento Kings.*

mother and traveled to the funeral without telling the
team. This angered the head coach, Brian Hill, who
threatened to suspend O'Neal.

"After my grandmother died, I was a twenty-four-
year-old kid trying to put all my feelings together," he

O'Neal prepares for a free throw, one of his biggest weaknesses.

said. "I was even considering taking a month off just to get my world straight. I left for the funeral on a Thursday, and we were playing the Bulls on a Sunday. I didn't call the Magic. They knew where I was. They knew what I was doing. But for some reason, they turned [it] into how unprofessional I was."[3] The situation led to O'Neal's unhappiness on the team.

Back on the basketball court, O'Neal and Orlando lost to the Chicago Bulls in the 1996 play-offs. It was the third year in a row their season ended in disappointment, and it marked the last time O'Neal wore a Magic uniform. That summer he became a **free agent**, which meant he could sign a contract with any team in the NBA.

CHAPTER FOUR

Building a Dynasty

O'Neal was named to Dream Team III for the 1996 Summer Olympics in Atlanta, Georgia. The team was made up of NBA superstars and was considered the greatest collection of basketball talent in the world. While in Atlanta practicing for the games, O'Neal rejected a new contract from the Magic and signed a deal instead with the Los Angeles Lakers. It was worth more than $120 million, making him the highest-paid player in the history of the NBA. After helping to lead the U.S. team to an undefeated record and a gold medal, O'Neal moved to Los Angeles to get ready for the 1996–1997 season.

Lakers fans were thrilled to have O'Neal on the team. The Lakers had not been in the NBA Finals in six years, and O'Neal was looking forward to leading the team to victory. But his first season in Los Angeles did not turn out as he and the Lakers' fans had hoped. O'Neal missed thirty-one games with injuries, including torn knee ligaments, and the Lakers were beaten in the second round of the play-offs. The season did have one shining moment for O'Neal, though. The NBA celebrated its fifty-year anniversary by naming the fifty greatest players in league history. At age twenty-five O'Neal was the youngest player to receive the honor.

Mr. Popular

Living in Los Angeles gave O'Neal the opportunity to continue his singing and acting careers. He created his own recording company called TWIsM (The World Is Mine) and released two more successful rap albums. On the movie screen he played a two-thousand-year-old genie in the movie *Kazaam*, which was popular with kids.

O'Neal also took time to help out within the community. He was a champion of children's causes and got involved with organizations that helped kids. He was a spokesman for the Boys and Girls Club and RIF (Reading Is Fundamental). At Christmas he became "Shaq-a-Claus" and bought toys for disadvantaged kids.

In the summer months, when O'Neal was not playing basketball, he took part in hosting instructional basketball clinics. He gave kids lessons not only in shooting and dribbling, but also in life. During one clinic he revealed the keys to his success when he told them, "The best thing that happened to me is I worked

*Together with Bill Gates (left), O'Neal launches the
online program called "Stay Safe Online."*

A proud O'Neal and his mother Lucille at his 2000 graduation from Louisiana State University.

hard, I listened to my parents, I stayed off drugs, and I stayed in school. That's why I'm here today."[4]

World Champions

When Michael Jordan retired from the NBA in 1998, O'Neal became the league's biggest star, and his popularity reached a new high. Despite his outstanding play he could not keep the Lakers from losing in the 1998 and 1999 play-offs. That was when the team decided to change coaches. They hired Phil Jackson, who had coached the Chicago Bulls to six NBA titles in the 1990s. Jackson preferred a team-oriented style of offense, meaning all five players had a chance to score.

Lakers coach Phil Jackson shakes O'Neal's hand after a Western Conference play-off game in 2000.

The goal was to take some of the pressure off O'Neal. The strategy worked as teammate Kobe Bryant emerged as an up-and-coming star. He and O'Neal played well together as the Lakers started to win under Jackson's leadership. One of the highlights of O'Neal's season was when he scored a career-best sixty-one points on March 6—his birthday. He finished the season averaging 29.7 points to lead the league in scoring.

Los Angeles ended the season at 67-15, the best record in the NBA. They beat all three opponents in the Western Conference play-offs to make it to the Fi-

NBA Commissioner David Stern (right) presents O'Neal with the Finals MVP Award in 2000.

nals at last. Facing the Indiana Pacers, O'Neal showed why he was considered the league's best player. He scored forty-one points in Game 6 to beat the Pacers and clinch the title. Finally an NBA champion after eight years in the league, O'Neal was overcome with emotion. He had proved his critics wrong. "The night I cried, I let go of a lot of the rage inside me," he said. "All the bad feelings I had toward the people who told me I couldn't do it sort of melted away."[5]

O'Neal averaged thirty-eight points and received the series MVP Award. Having already been named MVP of the regular season and the All-Star game, he became only the third player in NBA history to win all three awards in the same year.

Back-to-Back-to-Back Titles

After winning his first NBA title, O'Neal predicted to reporters the Lakers would repeat as champions the next year. But the 2000–2001 season did not start smoothly for the team. Bryant, who had become a league superstar the previous season, demanded the ball more, angering O'Neal. The two struggled for control of the team much of the season. They both spoke to reporters about their problems, and the story made national headlines. It looked as if their shaky relationship might cost the Lakers a chance to repeat as champions. The team finished with eleven fewer wins than they had their championship season. But by the start of the play-offs, the two stars mended their differences and the Lakers were back in winning form.

The team returned to the Finals, where they faced the Philadelphia 76ers. O'Neal proved to be unstoppable as he led the team to its second straight title. He was named MVP of the series.

In the 2001–2002 season O'Neal had another all-star season, averaging 27.2 points a game. But experts predicted the Lakers' reign was going to end. The team finished behind the Sacramento Kings in the regular season, and the Kings looked ready to win a championship. The play-offs again brought out the best in O'Neal and the team, though. Down three games to two against the Kings in the Western Conference Finals, O'Neal scored forty-one points in Game 6 to tie the series. In Game 7 he sank several important free throws as the Lakers won 112-106 in overtime. They advanced to the 2002 NBA Finals for the third year in a row.

Among the Greats

The Lakers played the New Jersey Nets, and O'Neal stayed at the top of his game. The Nets had no one who could stop him. He scored forty points in Game 2 while making twelve of fourteen free throws. For the series he averaged 36.2 points a game while leading the Lakers to a 4-0 sweep He was also named the MVP of the finals for the third straight year.

Experts already place O'Neal in a category that includes basketball's all-time greatest players, including Kareem Abdul-Jabbar, Wilt Chamberlain, and Michael Jordan. Although the spotlight is still shining brightly on O'Neal, who shows no signs of slowing down, he

Kobe Bryant (right) congratulates O'Neal on scoring a basket during a game.

Triumphant in victory, O'Neal hugs his stepfather after winning the NBA championship.

realizes the day is coming when he will have to call it quits. "I know that when I'm thirty-two and thirty-three, there will probably be a youngster coming in, twenty-four or twenty-five," he said. "He will have much more energy. Might even be a little bit bigger, a little bit better. Once it's time, it's not fun and I can't dominate anymore, then I'll be ready to give it to the next dominant big man."[6]

Notes

Chapter Two: Impact Player
1. O'Neal, *Shaq Talks Back*. New York: St. Martin's Press, 2001, p. 29.

Chapter Three: Magic Man
2. O'Neal, *Shaq Talks Back*, p. 2.
3. O'Neal, *Shaq Talks Back*, p. 45.

Chapter Four: Building a Dynasty
4. Bruce Hunter, *Shaq Impaq*. Chicago: Bonus Books, 1993, p. 53.
5. O'Neal, *Shaq Talks Back*, p. 254.
6. O'Neal, *Shaq Talks Back*, p. 258.

Glossary

all-American: An award given to the best college athletes in the nation.

center: Usually the tallest basketball player on the team. He or she plays close to the basket.

Division I: The highest level of competition in college sports. Division II is second highest, followed by Division III.

drill sergeant: An officer in the army who trains new soldiers.

foul: Occurs when a player hits or illegally blocks another player.

free agent: A professional player who is not under contract and is free to sign with another team.

free throw: A shot from the free throw line that occurs after a foul.

Most Valuable Player Award: An award given to the most important player on his or her team.

rebound: Occurs when a player gains possession of the ball after a missed shot.

For Further Exploration

Books

Bill Gutman, *Shaquille O'Neal: A Biography*. New York: Archway Paperbacks, 1993. Includes information about O'Neal's high school and college careers and his rookie season with the Orlando Magic.

Paul Joseph, *Awesome Athletes: Shaquille O'Neal*. Edina, MN: Abdo & Daughters, 1997. Examines O'Neal's experiences on and off the basketball court. Also includes a timeline of his basketball accomplishments.

Michael J. Sullivan, *Sports Great: Shaquille O'Neal*. Springfield, NJ: Enslow, 1995. A biography of the NBA's premier center. Provides college and professional statistics.

Tim Ungs, *Basketball Legends: Shaquille O'Neal*. New York: Chelsea House, 1997. Details the all-star center's personal life and pro career, and gives statistics through the 1995–1996 season.

Internet Sources

ESPN.com, "Shaquille O'Neal." http://sports.espn.go. com. An excellent resource for O'Neal's current statistics.

NBA.com, "Shaquille O'Neal Player Info." www.nba.com. Includes career highlights, game-by-game statistics, a career biography, and more.

Website

Shaquille O'Neal's Official Basketball Website (www.shaq.com). Includes NBA news, a game schedule, O'Neal's off-court interests, and photographs.

Index

Picture Credits

About the Author

Raymond H. Miller is the author of more than fifty nonfiction books for children. He has written on a range of topics from sports trivia to fossilized shark teeth. Miller enjoys playing sports and spending time outdoors with his wife and two daughters.